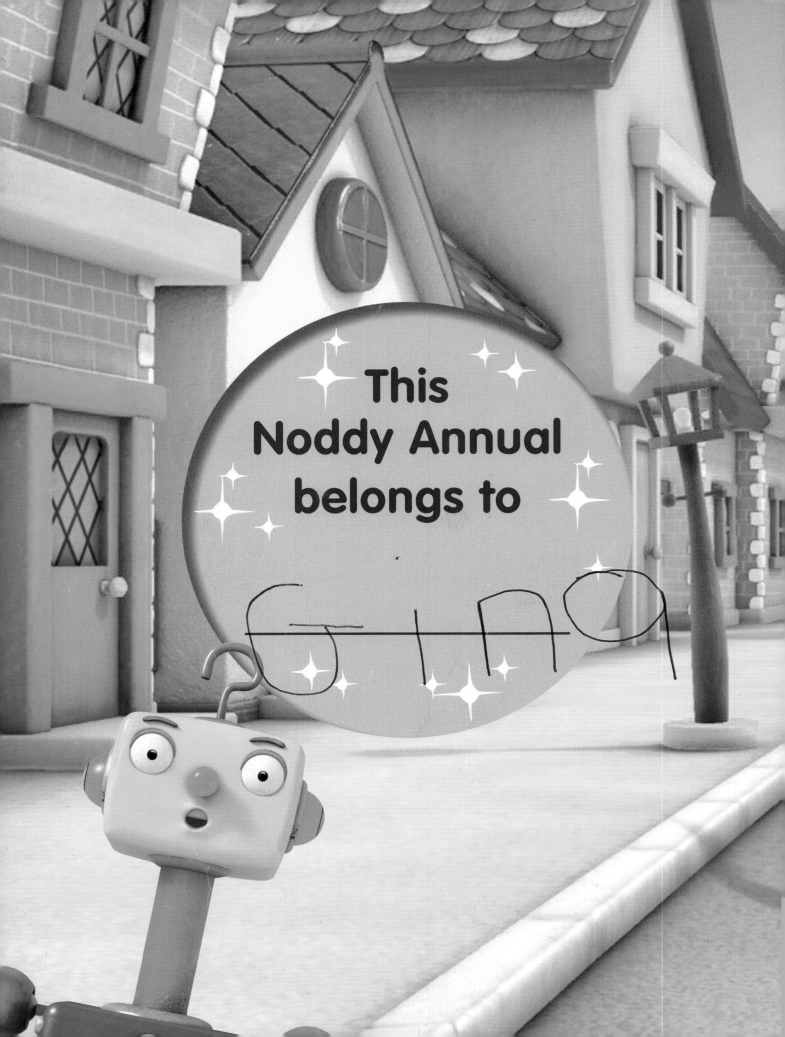

This
Noddy Annual
belongs to

Gina

Contents

EGMONT
We bring stories to life

First published in Great Britain in 2009
by Egmont UK Limited
239 Kensington High Street, London W8 6SA

Created for Egmont by Ruby Shoes Limited.
Written by Brenda Apsley.
Designed by Nicola Meidlinger.

NODDY® TOYLAND® NODDY IN TOYLAND™ copyright © 2009
Chorion Rights Limited. All rights reserved.

ISBN 978 1 4052 4723 8
1 3 5 7 9 10 8 6 4 2
Printed in Italy

Hello!

I'm Noddy, and this is my friend, Bumpy Dog. We live in Toyland, where we have lots of adventures. We're always ready to play and have fun, and we hope you are too!

ARE YOU READY

TO PLAY?

Welcome to Toy Town!

Toy Town is a magical place where fun and adventures happen every day!

Noddy drives around in Car. When he hears Car's horn go beep, beep, Noddy knows that something is wrong, or someone needs his help.

Noddy lives in a little house made of building blocks. He loves adventures, and when things go wrong, he always tries to put them right.

Read about the four friends, then try to answer these questions.

1 Who lives in a kennel outside Noddy's house?

2 Who lives in a toadstool?

3 Who lives in a house made of building blocks?

4 Whose horn goes beep, beep?

Noddy's friend **Big Ears** lives in a toadstool on the edge of the Enchanted Wood. He always has stories to tell, and a little magic to sprinkle around.

Bumpy Dog is lots of fun! He lives in a kennel at the side of Noddy's house, and he loves running around, playing ... and digging!

Answers: 1. Bumpy Dog; 2. Big Ears; 3. Noddy; 4. Car.

Toy Town Friends

Noddy has lots of friends in Toy Town!

MR PLOD

LINDEN BERRY

THE SKITTLES

WHIZ

Can you answer these questions?
1 Who has wings?
2 Who wears a pink hair bow?
3 Who wears roller skates?

JUMBO

MR WOBBLY MAN

TESSIE BEAR

MR BEETLE

CLOCKWORK MOUSE

Ready to Play

Noddy and his friends are always ready to play. Join in their game of Hide and Seek by helping Noddy find his friends.

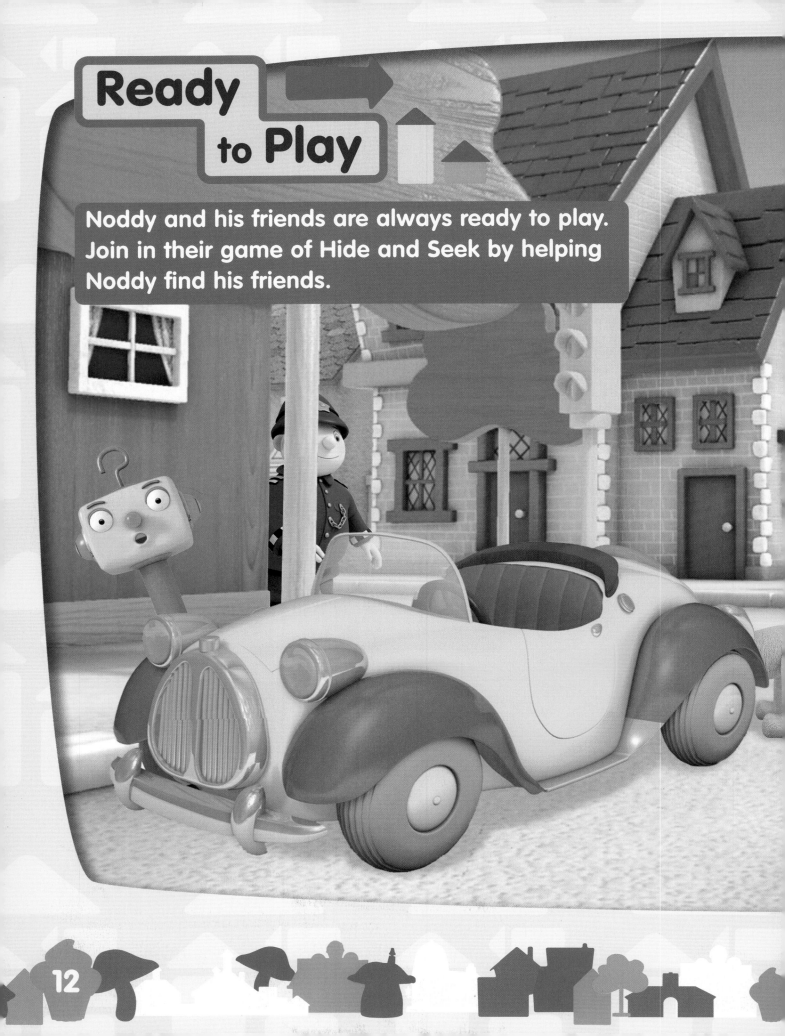

How many of Noddy's friends can you see?

Circle each friend you find.
Do you know their names?

Answer: 6 of Noddy's friends are hiding. Their names are Whiz, Jumbo, Bumpy Dog, Big Ears, Mr Plod and Linden Berry.

Tessie Bear's Picnic Pies

Tessie Bear has made lots of googleberry pies for the Toy Town Picnic. But as usual, Sly and Gobbo always try and spoil the fun!

Which plate of pies have the naughty goblins been gobbling?

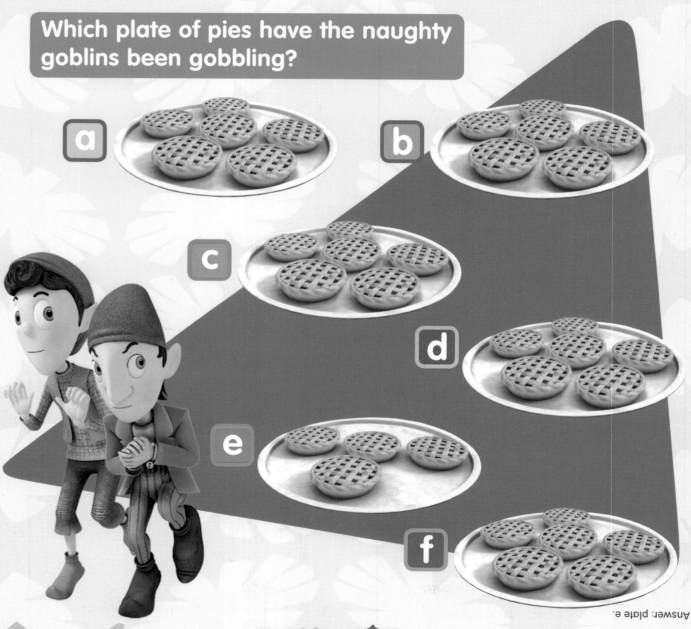

Answer: plate e.

14

Magic!

Big Ears' magic sometimes goes wrong!
One day, he tried to get rid of the mud on
Bumpy Dog, but made Bumpy vanish, too!

Help Big Ears make Bumpy appear again,
by drawing and colouring in his picture.

Noddy and the Magic Paintbrush

One day, Noddy was throwing sticks for Bumpy Dog to fetch.

When it was time for Noddy to go to visit Big Ears, Bumpy Dog wanted to carry on playing.

"You want me to throw another stick, do you?" said Noddy. "All right, but this is the last one!"

Noddy threw the stick, but it bounced off a flower, and hit Car's door!

The stick scratched Car's shiny yellow paint. "Sorry, Car," said Noddy. "We'll go to see Whiz. He'll be able to fix it."

But when Car, Noddy and Bumpy Dog got to the Garage, Whiz was nowhere to be seen.

"Hello, Lindy," said Noddy. "Is Whiz here? I need him to fix Car's door for me."

Lindy shook her head. "I'm sorry, Whiz is out," she told Noddy. "But he's left me in charge. I can fix Car's door for you."

Lindy is rather untidy, so things were in a bit of a mess!

"I'm sorting everything out," she explained. "The yellow paint should be in the yellow pile. Look, here it is."

But Lindy painted Car's door blue and green, not yellow!

"Sorry," she said. "Shall I use fairy magic to fix Car?"

"No," said Noddy. "Whiz doesn't like it when you use magic to fix things. I'll see if Big Ears can help."

Big Ears didn't have any yellow paint – but he did have a Magic Paintbrush, which painted Car's door yellow!

Noddy and Big Ears went to the Jelly Bowl for tea. They left the Magic Paintbrush outside, in a flower pot, but it ran away!

"Come on, Car," said Noddy when he saw that it was gone. "Catch that paintbrush!"

Soon, Toy Town was covered in splashes and splodges of paint! The Jelly Bowl was green, with big blue spots, and the Magic Paintbrush even tried to paint the little Skittles!

"Oh, dear!" said Noddy.

"Something must be done!" said Mr Plod.

Noddy agreed. "It's our fault that the Magic Paintbrush is here making trouble," he said. "So Big Ears and I will catch it."

Noddy and Big Ears soon found the Magic Paintbrush.

"But how do we make it stop?" asked Noddy.

"I can't remember," said Big Ears.

"I'll fetch my Magic Book to find out."

That gave Noddy an idea! "Fetch!" he said.

"Fetch, Bumpy! Fetch the Magic Paintbrush!"

Bumpy Dog soon caught the Magic Paintbrush and gave it to Noddy. Clever Bumpy!

"I wonder if I can magic Toy Town back to the way it was?" said Big Ears.

"Who needs magic?" cried Noddy. "Let's get some proper paintbrushes and repaint Toy Town together! I'll ask Tessie Bear to make a picnic for us!"

"Woof, woof!" barked Bumpy Dog. Cakes, buns, cookies and, best of all, jelly! He liked the sound of that!

Toy Soldiers

"Face the front!" Major Noddy tells his toy soldiers. But some soldiers do not do as they are told!

Which soldiers are not facing the front? Tick ✔ the boxes.

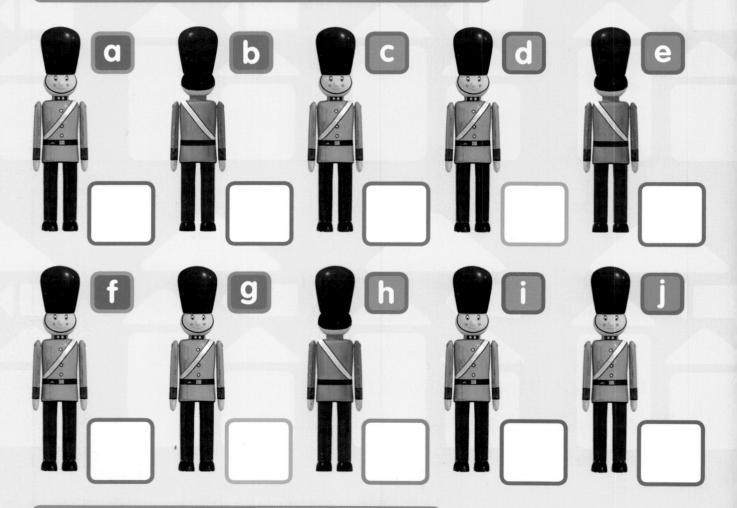

a   b   c   d   e

f   g   h   i   j

Now count the soldiers. How many are there altogether?

Answers: soldiers b, e and h are not facing the front; there are 10 soldiers.

22

Whiz's Garage

Whiz likes to keep his Garage neat and tidy, with all his tools in the right places.

Find the odd tool out in each row.

1

a   b   c   d

2

a   b   c   d

3

a   b   c   d

Answers: 1.b, 2.d, 3.a.

23

True or False?

Read about Noddy. Tick ✔ the things that are true, and cross ✘ the things that are false.

1 Sly is Noddy's best friend.

2 Whiz is the Toy Town policeman.

3 Big Ears lives in a toadstool.

4 Noddy's dog is called Barky Dog.

5 Tessie Bear's car is purple.

6 Noddy has a pompom on the end of his hat.

7 Whiz is a robot.

8 Noddy's car is red and blue.

9 Gobbo is a goblin.

10 Jumbo is a lion.

Bumpy Dog's Bones

Bumpy Dog has hidden some bones, but he's forgotten where!

How many can you find for him?

Answer: there are 7 bones.

Wibble, Wobble!

Here comes Mr Wobbly Man with the Jelly Bowl menu.

Circle the treats you'd like to eat! Which is your favourite?

Smile, Please!

Noddy loves his new camera! He used it to take this photo of his Toy Town friends.

Which of Noddy's friends can you see in the big photo opposite?

Tick ✔ the ones you can see, and cross ✗ the ones you can't.

a

b

c

d

e

f

g

h

Answer: pictures b, d, e, g and h can all be found in the big photo.

29

Linden Berry

Linden Berry the fairy loves doing the messiest, dirtiest, oiliest jobs at Whiz's Garage.

Tick ✓ **ONLY the tools Lindy uses to fix things.**

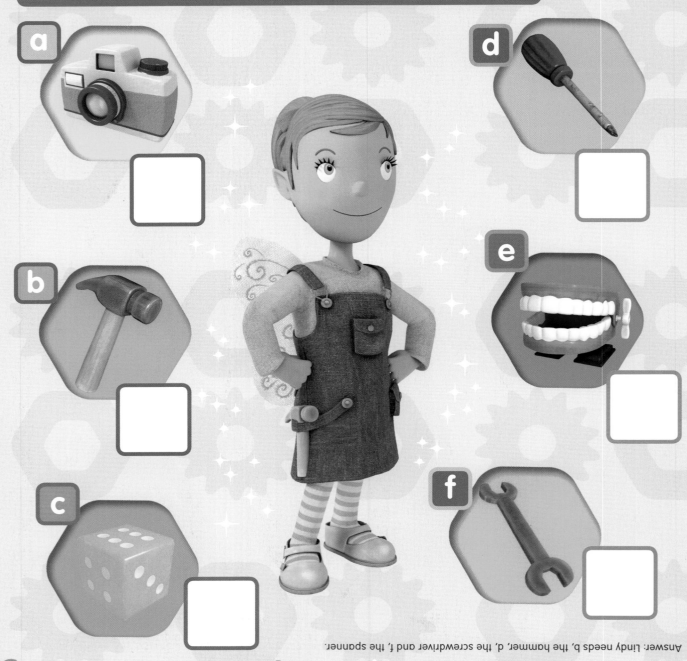

a ☐

b ☐

c ☐

d ☐

e ☐

f ☐

Answer: Lindy needs b, the hammer, d, the screwdriver and f, the spanner.

30

Happy Birthday, Tessie Bear!

Lucky Tessie Bear has a birthday present that matches her dress!

Draw and colour in something she would like to find inside the present. Now write **Tessie Bear** and your name on the gift tag.

to _____

from _____

Noddy and the Remote Control

One day, Mr Wobbly Man lost the remote control for his jelly mixer. Without it, he couldn't make jellies for the Jelly Bowl!

"Don't worry," said Noddy. "I'll get a new one from Whiz."

Whiz gave Noddy the control-it-all remote control he had just made, and Noddy took it home to test it.

Noddy pressed a button on the remote control, and the vacuum cleaner started working. "It works!" he cried.

While Noddy phoned Whiz to tell him that the remote control was working, naughty Bumpy Dog grabbed it, and ran off with it!

"Naughty Bumpy! Come back here!" cried Noddy. "Let's go, Car! We have to catch him!"

"Woof, woof!" barked Bumpy Dog. He loves chasing games, so he jumped on to the little remote control car and raced off to Toy Town as fast as he could go.

When Bumpy got there, he pressed the buttons on the remote control and made all sorts of odd things happen!

The door of the jail opened by itself, and the traffic lights stopped working!

"Tee, hee! Very peculiar!" laughed Mr Plod.

Noddy and Car caught up with Bumpy Dog at Whiz's Garage. Odd things were happening there, too!

"Help! The remote control is controlling meeee!" cried Whiz, whizzing around.

Noddy spoke to Bumpy. "Mr Wobbly Man needs the remote control to make his jelly mixer work," he said.

"Woof, woof!" barked Bumpy Dog, as he raced off.

At the Jelly Bowl, Noddy got Bumpy Dog to jump on the buttons of the remote control.

When Bumpy pressed the right one, the jelly mixer started working again!

Noddy squirted jelly out of a hosepipe on to the road, and it was so sticky that it stopped the little car.

"Thank you, Noddy. Thank you, Bumpy Dog!" said Mr Wobbly Man. "Now I can make jellies for everyone!"

Bumpy Dog wagged his tail happily. He just loves jelly!

Answer these questions about the story by ticking ✔ the right pictures.

1 Who gave Noddy a new remote control?

Whiz ⭘ Lindy ⭘ Mr Plod ⭘

2 Who said, "Tee, hee! Very peculiar!"?

Mr Plod ⭘ Tessie Bear ⭘ Whiz ⭘

3 Who just loves jelly?

Noddy ⭘ Bumpy Dog ⭘ Mr Plod ⭘

Answers: 1. Whiz, 2. Mr Plod, 3. Bumpy Dog.

Tell a Story

Now help tell Noddy's Remote Control story. Listen to the words and when you come to a picture, say the name.

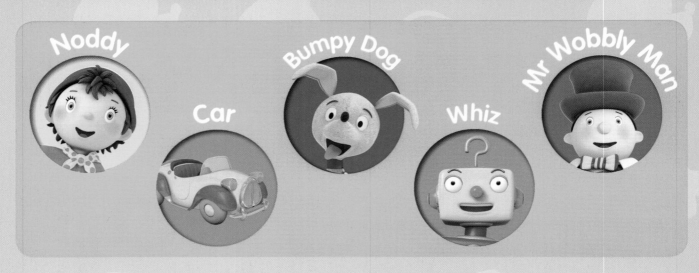

Noddy

Car

Bumpy Dog

Whiz

Mr Wobbly Man

One day, [Noddy] goes to see [Mr Wobbly Man] at the

Jelly Bowl. "Help, [Noddy]!" says [Mr Wobbly Man]. "I have

lost the remote control for my jelly mixer!"

"No jelly mixer means no jelly!" says  .

"  will know what to do. Come on,  ,

we need to go to the Garage!"  gives

 the new remote control he has made. "It

can control any gadget," says  . But when

 gets home,  runs off with it!

 goes to the Garage. The remote control

makes everything whiz and buzz – even  !

 and  follow  to the Jelly

Bowl. Clever  tells  that it is fun

to jump on the remote control, so  jumps on

the buttons. "That's right,  !" says  .

 pushes the right button. "My jelly mixer

is working again!" says . "Thank you,

. Thank you, ."  has a

reward for  and  and .

 knows what it is! Can you guess?

"Bzzz, jelly," says . "Woof!" says .

Count with Noddy

Noddy likes counting the spots on his dominoes.

Count the spots and tick ✔ the right answers.

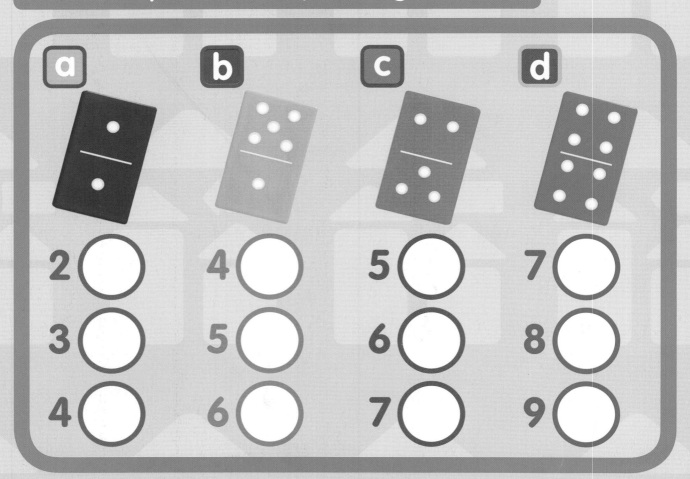

	a	b	c	d
	2 ◯	4 ◯	5 ◯	7 ◯
	3 ◯	5 ◯	6 ◯	8 ◯
	4 ◯	6 ◯	7 ◯	9 ◯

Find the Names

Can you find the names of Noddy and some of his friends hidden in the puzzle? They are spelled out across, from left to right ➡ or down, from top to bottom ⬇.

M	L	I	N	D	Y
P	V	X	M	Z	X
R	J	H	R	O	W
B	U	M	P	Y	H
Q	M	E	L	B	I
G	B	F	O	C	Z
N	O	D	D	Y	B

Tick ✔ a name when you find it.

NODDY ◯   BUMPY ◯   JUMBO ◯

WHIZ ◯   LINDY ◯   MR PLOD ◯

Hello Toy Town!

Noddy can see the whole of Toy Town when he flies over the rooftops in his little plane.

Who can Noddy spot? Tick ✔ ONLY the friends he can see.

Tessie Bear

Mr Plod

Whiz

Mr Wobbly Man

Spot the Difference

Would you like to live in a house like Noddy's, with a big slide bed in it?

These pictures look the same but 5 things are different in picture 2.

Can you spot them all?

1

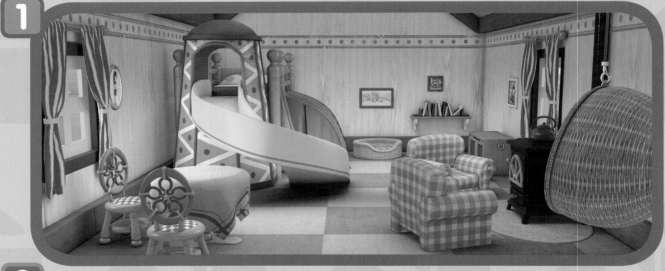

2

Answers: Bumpy Dog, a football and a jelly have been added, the books are missing and an armchair is a different colour.

46

Red, Blue and Yellow

Can you guess what Noddy's favourite colours are? Yes, red, blue and yellow!

Answer these questions by drawing a circle around the right colours.

1 What colour is Noddy's hat?

2 What colour are the spots on Noddy's scarf?

3 What colour is Noddy's belt?

4 What colour is Noddy's top?

5 What colour are Noddy's shorts?

Answers: 1. blue, 2. red, 3. yellow, 4. red, 5. blue.

Clever Car!

When Noddy has to drive over rough, bumpy ground, Car can be fitted with big monster wheels. "Clever Car!" says Noddy.

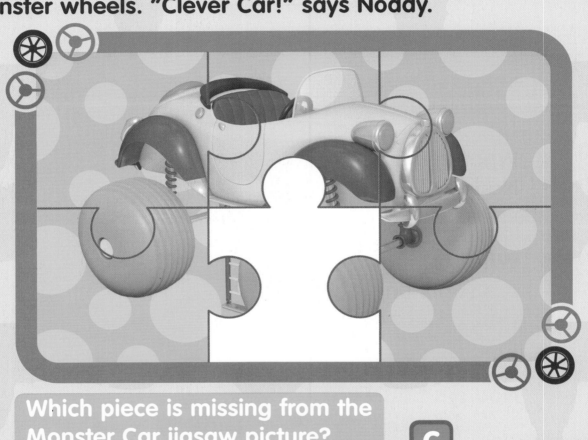

Which piece is missing from the Monster Car jigsaw picture?

a

b

c

48

When Noddy needs to travel over water, Car becomes a hover car that floats on the waves. "Clever Car!" says Noddy.

Which piece is missing from the Hover Car jigsaw picture?

a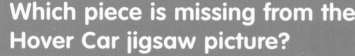

b

c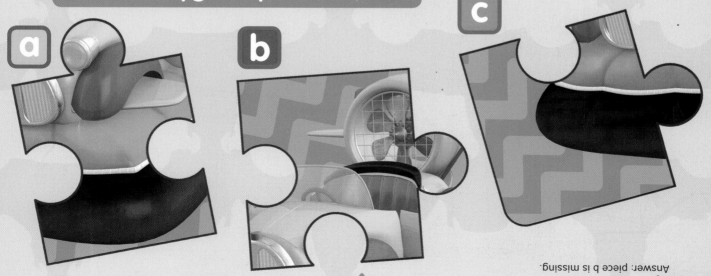

49

Sly and Gobbo

Sly and Gobbo's Goblin Rule Number One is always try and spoil the fun. Naughty goblins!

Which picture of Sly and Gobbo is the odd one out?

a

b

c

d

The Skittle Family

Mrs Skittle has lots of knock-me-down children who just love falling over!

Count the little Skittles, then colour in the right number.

1 2 3 4
5 6 7 8

Answer: there are 6 little Skittles.

Noddy Goes to Toy Town

There are lots and lots of houses in Toy Town, and they are painted in all kinds of colours! Draw lines to match the houses that are exactly the same.

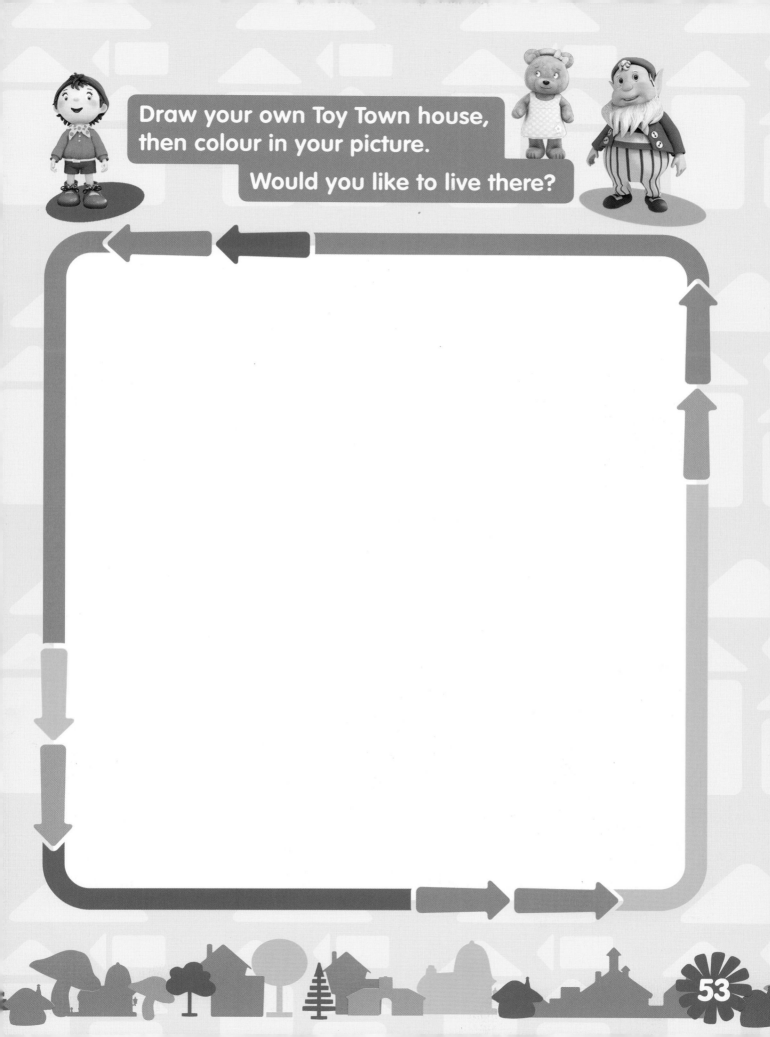

Draw your own Toy Town house, then colour in your picture.

Would you like to live there?

Clockwork Mouse

Clockwork Mouse is one of Noddy's best friends. Noddy turns his key to wind him up when he feels run down.

Can you match Clockwork Mouse to his shadow?

Answer: shadow d matches Clockwork Mouse.

Happy Birthday to Noddy!

Noddy loves it when the postman brings lots of cards on his birthday. It's a happy start to a happy day!

Draw and colour in a special card to send to Noddy, then write your name on the line.

from _Oliver_

This Way, Mr Beetle!

Mr Beetle needs to put some petrol in his car.

Can you show him the quickest way through the maze of streets to get to Whiz's Garage?

RACE TRACK

WHIZ'S GARAGE

Noddy's House

Lucky Noddy lives in a house made of building blocks.

Find these building blocks in the picture, and use the same colours to colour them in.

a

b

c

Answers: a. blue; b. green; c. blue.

Mr Plod Loses his Laugh

Noddy, Tessie Bear and Bumpy Dog were very pleased when the first of their Chattering Teeth friends arrived in Toy Town!

Chitter-chatter, went the Chattering Teeth, jumping up and down.

"Let's be Chattering Teeth!" cried Noddy, doing little jumps.

"That looks like funny business," said Mr Plod when he saw Noddy and Tessie Bear jumping around like Chattering Teeth. "Tee, hee! Ha, ha, ha!"

"Play Chattering Teeth with us, Mr Plod," said Noddy. "It's fun!"

But Mr Plod was laughing too much to chatter! "I know, let's play No Laughing Allowed," he said. "The winner is the last one to laugh!"

Noddy and Tessie Bear soon laughed, and Mr Plod won the game. But he didn't look very pleased about it.

"You can laugh now," said Tessie Bear.

"No, I can't," said Mr Plod. "I've lost my laugh!"

"Don't worry, Mr Plod, we'll help you find it!" said Noddy.

Noddy and Tessie Bear jumped around and pulled their best silly faces, but Mr Plod didn't even smile.

Noddy and Tessie tickled Mr Plod with feathers, but that didn't work, either.

"It's not working, is it, Mr Plod?" said Noddy. "I know, we'll take you to the Jelly Bowl. It's the funniest place in Toy Town, and Mr Wobbly Man is sure to make you laugh!"

When Mr Wobbly Man came out of the Jelly Bowl with a double googleberry jelly sundae, he wibbled, then he wobbled, and the sundae ended up all over Noddy!

That made everyone laugh ... everyone except poor Mr Plod.

"I don't think I'm ever going to laugh again," he said sadly. "I'm going home."

"We need a Big Noddy Plan," said Noddy. He thought hard and soon he knew just what to do!

Noddy asked the Chattering Teeth and all his other friends to help.
"Can you all chitter-chatter?" he asked his friends, and they all nodded, and jumped around like Chattering Teeth!

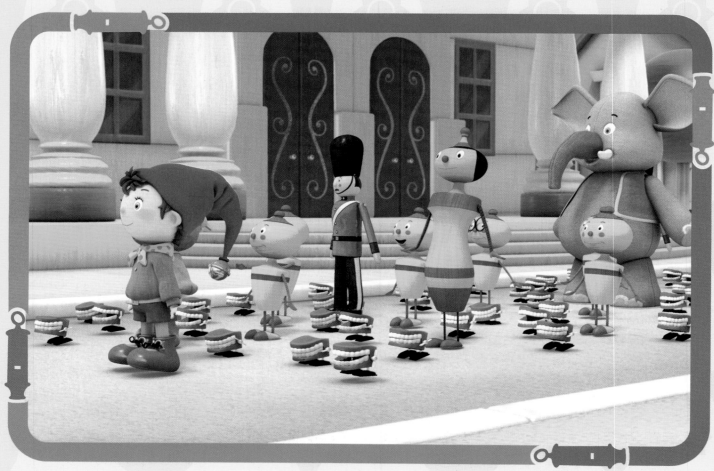

"Good," said Noddy, marching off. "Now follow me!"
When Noddy and his friends marched to the Police Station, Mr Plod smiled a big smile. "A chattering parade!" he said. "That's very funny! Hilarious!"

"Mr Plod's laugh is almost back now," said Noddy. "One more funny thing, and he'll laugh as he always did."

Then Bumpy Dog bumped into Noddy and knocked him over – bump! – that did the trick!

"Ho, ho, ho!" laughed Mr Plod. "Hee, hee, hee! That was very funny, Noddy!"

Mr Plod laughed and laughed until his sides were sore. "Oooo!" he giggled. "Ha-ha-ha-ha. I've – ooooh – aaaaah – tee-hee-hee, I've got my laugh back! Thank you, Noddy!"

Spot the Difference

When cars and machines break down,
Whiz fixes them in his Garage.

1

These pictures look the same but 5 things are different in picture 2. Can you spot them all?

2

Noddy's Questions

"Can you answer these questions about my friends?" asks Noddy.

1 Who lives in the Picnic Basket? Is it:
a Big Ears
b Whiz, or
c Tessie Bear?

2 Which of my friends drives this blue sports car?

3 Where does Linden Berry work?

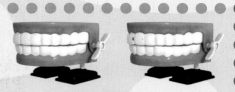

4 Who is this? Is it:
a Mr Wobbly Man
b Mr Beetle, or
c Mr Plod?

5 Who lives in this house?

"Check the answers to see how many questions you got right, then write your score here," says Noddy.

"Well done! Write your name on the line."

Clever _____

knows all about Noddy and his friends!

Butterflies!

Woof, woof! **Bumpy Dog loves chasing games!**

Colour in a butterfly for each one you can see in the big picture. Then count them, and write the number.

All your favourite friends from Toyland!

Look out for the new range of toys, based on the **Noddy in Toyland** TV show. Includes plush, vehicles, Noddy House playset and much, much more!

www.noddy.com

BAN DAI

Bandai UK Limited
t: 01489-790944
www.bandai.co.uk